Mary Eliza Perine Tucker

Loew's bridge, a Broadway idyl

Mary Eliza Perine Tucker

Loew's bridge, a Broadway idyl

ISBN/EAN: 9783744677561

Printed in Europe, USA, Canada, Australia, Japan

Cover: Foto ©Andreas Hilbeck / pixelio.de

More available books at **www.hansebooks.com**

A

BROADWAY IDYL.

———— ✦ ◦ ✦ ————

NEW YORK:

M. DOOLADY, PUBLISHER,

448 BROOME STREET.

1867.

JOHN J. REED, PRINTER AND STEREOTYPER,
43 Centre Street, New York.

A BROADWAY IDYL.

FOR hours I stood upon THE BRIDGE, (¹)

Which looms like a volcanic ridge,

    Above a scathing fire below.

A flaming crater of burning hearts—

And, as souls passed beneath my feet,

As weary souls passed to and fro

A knowledge came, so sad, yet sweet,

    Each inner life I seemed to know.

Oh, heaven and earth! the sins and sorrows

That scarred each heart with countless furrows!

And yet I had a glimpse of love;

For maidens, pure as snow-white dove

　　　　And innocent of guile,

All heedless of this world of pain,

　　　　Passed under with a smile.

Bright rosy cheeks, the badge of health—

　　　　Eyes dancing in their mirth—

And rose-bud lips as yet unpressed,

Soft golden hair, by none caressed,

　　　　For save the passion born at birth,

And vanity the sin of wealth,

 Their hearts were pure, free of the lust,

 Which aye debases mortal dust.

And faces sweet as Poet's dream,

Sad as the fair Evangeline,

Or like Maud Muller. by the stream

 In the meadows raking hay,

Whose face betrays the " vague unrest "

Which drives from every human breast

 All happiness away.

Some seeking for their "Gabriel,"

Some mourning for lost " Judge."

Some hiding 'neath a smiling face
    The sorrow I know well,
The sorrow which makes hearts but graves,
    And faces monuments.

Full many a floweret passed beneath,
    Clasping the hand of sin,
And childish voices in merry glee,
    Made musical the din,
Like some sweet symphony which swells
    Amid the noise on battle field,
Waking, in many a heart, the wells
    Of some emotion

A BROADWAY IDYL.

Long since dead to all save One
Who for us gave His only Son ;
    And over me a softness crept,
    And pining for my own, I wept.

Thank God for children! for they give
New life to those who would not live,
But that the bonds, so holy bound.
Like some fresh vine, an oak around
Their aching hearts, too full of grief,
Which find in bondage sweet relief.
God bless each childish happy face,
Each fairy form so full of grace—

For without children life would be

  Devoid of all its purity.

An angel? No, 'tis but a child of earth.

But Venus smiled at that fair maiden's birth.

True, Poverty has placed on her his mark

  Of scanty garments—

But tattered robes hide not the wealth and

  grace

That nature showered on hair, and form, and

  face.

Full many a childless parent would bestow

Gold, yellow glittering gold, could that fair child

With her pure face, by art's hand undefiled,

    Have been her very own.

But Nature sells not, freely does she give,

God in His wisdom, that we all may live

    Contented with our lot,

Gives mind and beauty to His favored few,

To some He grants more than their meed of

    wealth,

And to the rest He opes His store of health.

This child is leading by her gentle hand

    Her aged grandsire, on whose sightless eyes

The hand of Time has placed his seal of seals.

Nor will they open, until in the skies

Light of all light His glorious self reveals.

On, on they pass—but ah ! that piercing scream

Awakes me—is it but a dream ?

No ! there he stands in middle of Broadway

A frozen statue, moving neither way.

A horse is near him, and with instinct rare

The little child, who makes his life her care,

As if to shield him from approaching harm,

Twines her fair arms about his aged form.

I hold my breath; but ah, no need of fear,

The watchful guardian of the Bridge (²) is near,

Robed in his blue coat, with the star of gold,

Whose courage gives him mine of strength un-

t)ld ;

He hurls the horse back, and they onward move,

The loving guided by the hand of love.

A rag-man passes, clad in vesture poor.

O scorn him not, for in his dirty bag

Is many a space for thoughts to rest upon—

Of countless value is each little rag :

Like trifles they accumulate,

And when they mingle into one,

By trying process changing state,

Upon their surface lurks the hate

    Or love. of many a nation.

'Tis well we think not. as we cast aside

The tiny fragments of our daily task,

Of the dread tidings those same rags may bring

    E'en to our door.

Some great man's fate, like Maximilian's doom,

May o'er even strangers cast a death-like gloom.

Some unjust act, a NATION put to shame,

Some lines of praise. but pages full of blame.

Praise give to poets, for 'tis poets' due,—

Worth should be granted to the rag-man too,

For in his hands the firm foundation lies,

Upon which poets' airy-castles rise.

Down, down from Romance's perch, my muse,

Wipe Fancy's dust from off thy shoes:

Let good and pure rest for a while,

Portray realities of guile.

Guile? Say, is there real guilt on earth?

    And shall we all be judged

By sins—not weakness?

    God forbid!

Mortals we are, conceived in sin—

None, none are pure, all " might have been,"

Had woman's heart been made of stone.

All, all are frail, and she who passes now

With stains of sin upon her pallid brow,

And misery untold within her heart,

I leave to Him who said,

" Neither do I condemn thee, go thy way

And sin no more," for what art thou but clay !

Weary and slow she passes 'neath the arch,

And now, upon her face I see a flush, as if her

youth

Had been renewed by some glad truth,

As glancing up, into a manly face.

She speaks her greeting with a pleading grace.

No word from him: naught save a smile of

      scorn!

Alone she stands—he with the tide moves **on.**

All color from the flushing cheeks now dies,

Hands press her heart to stifle woe's deep cries.

And onward, moved by demon of despair,

She braves the " king of terrors " in his lair.

Say, is she saved? Will the grim spectre,

      Death,

Take from her more than life's short fleeting

      breath?

Doom her to endless misery of mind,

    Leaving a tainted name behind?

Men swell the current,—many of them wear

Upon their brows the cruel badge of care.

The magic Greenback, like some rolling ball,

Gathers the man-moss, hurls them into "Wall."(³)

Each eager face in passing seems to say—

" Chasing a dollar, comrades, clear the way!

I am ambitious, and I fain would win :

Would gain the dollar even if I sin."

And oft, alas, in raging lust for gold,

Life's cup is broken, and a soul is sold!

Some push along with satisfaction's air,

While others wear the visage of despair.

Some, looking forward, in perspective see

When their one dollar shall ten thousand be.

Some glancing upward, building in the sky

Bright airy castles soon to fade and die :

While sad-faced men look backward and pass on

Cursing the day that ever they were born.

For empty pockets begets woes untold,

And friends and comfort vanish with our gold.

Then should we wonder that the trash is sought,

With which e'en friendship is oft sold and

bought ?

There, mark the difference in the prosperous man,

And one who gains existence as he can—

One with his head erect, the other bowed,

The poor are humble, but the rich are proud.

Hark! surely there is music in the air!

　　'Tis "Dixie" floating on this Northern breeze,

Thrilling each Southern heart with thoughts

　　Of a lost Nation's hope, and her despair.

This world is strange, 'tis an anomaly!

For glancing downward now I see

A one-armed soldier, in a coat of blue—

And, by-the-by, his legs are missing too.

Grinding with his one hand the "Dixie" song.

Perchance, who knows, that very tune was
played,

When in the midst of some mad martial raid
The missile came along

Which left of noble manhood but the wreck.

Now, standing by his side, is one
I know, a warrior, brave for Southern rights:
All strife is ended, and all warring done.
And the blue-clad soldier's eyes seem dancing
lights,
As in his hand the Southern warrior places

His mite ; true, 'tis a small donation,

But it betrays the great appreciation

    Of a brave soul, for spirit kindred born.(4)

Now " Yankee Doodle " falls upon my ear,

Then " Erin's Wearing of the Green " I hear ;

And as the human current moves along,

I read their Nation as each hears the song—

For faces speak, and eyes will tell the truth :

When Memory, with swift electric string,

Draws Past to Present, on sweet music's wing.

A tear in manhood's eye is no disgrace,

And pity lends a charm to every face.

Statesmen, the satellites of Fame,

Are mingling with the throng,

Some heart sore with a Nation's blame,

Some charmed by the Siren song

Of present popularity.

Ah me! how changes tide with time.

Public opinion is as vacillating

As seasons are, forever on the change,

Warm, temperate, cold, in changing only true,

Or like some serpent, with its roseate hue,

Of commendation, luring on its victim

E'en to death; who, wounded by the sting

Of misconception, like the poor snail,

Shrinks in his shell, and starving for fame,

    Dies in obscurity.

New eyes are mine—I see as ne'er before;

Not forms alone, as in the days of yore,

But acts—sins long untold—

And acts of mercy to my gaze unfold.

    I see too, lives of men,

And step by step, I trace some back to when

With ragged jacket, hatless head, and feet

Frozen and bare, they wandered in the street.

With hope, ambition, faith within their hearts,

    Whose dirty faces bore the stamp of MAN.

God's own insignia, neither wealth nor fame,

Nor right by birth to high ancestral name,

     Can grant such priceless boon.

The glory be to him who can declare

I am the founder of the name I bear.

Not the last scion of the great of earth,

But first : the hour which gave me birth

Shall be remembered, until time shall be

     Lost in the mazes of Eternity.

One word of praise, and it is nobly won

For him who said, " I will win for my Son

     A name all glorious and bright."(5)

Censorious world! oh why not o'er the past

Oblivion's vail in its soft darkness cast

    And honor grant, for what one is not was.

Our City rulers pass in grand array.

Some whose each step pollutes this snowy way,

Whose nervous glances tell that they have sold

Their honor for position and for gold.

Others, whose pure lives can command

Respect, aye love, of all e'en in this land,

    Where merit's granted but to favored few.

Our present Mayor, with abstracted air,

Comes with kind greeting, for high, low and fair.

In each heart holds he a much envied place,

And his position fills with nameless grace.

And yet he bears upon his brow the badge

Of hope deferred, Ambition's goal half won—

The race for station only just begun.[6]

His rival follows, and determination

Within his eye shows will to do, or dare—

Not only will, but power,

Dame Nature's priceless dower.

From very foot the mount of fame he trod :

Sprung from the people, he's the people's god.[7]

And Authors, too, the devils of the quill,

Who daily, hourly their poor brains distil:

Exalted, trampled by the public will;

And yet they cater, and will cater still,

Undaunted by the missiles hurled

       Each day by a censorious world.

Some with their faces beaming bright

See in their eyes success' light;

Some who on yesterday were naught,

To-day they find themselves the sought

And courted, for their genius bright,

       A reputation

       Made by the " NATION,"

Growing like Jonah's gourd all in a night.

And some poor sinner who awoke

From dream of fame, alas to find

His fancy's child, child of his mind,

Damned by the critics,

       Or unnoticed passed.

Ah, well, when he is dead, perchance his name

May live forever, immortalized by fame.

Such is the world's great largess to the dead,

The genius who when living wanted bread.

'Tis marvellous how mortals can invent

The ways and means to increase worldly stores.

Scorn not beginnings, and each small thing prize,

From e'en a cord.(°) sometimes large fortunes

    rise.

Yon apple-woman, vender of small wares,

Stale lozenges, fruit, candy, and vile cakes,

Who sells to urchins pennies' worth of aches,

Has now the gold safe hoarded in the bank,

With which to buy high place in fashion's rank.

Merit is nothing, money rules the day

Right royally, with rare despotic sway.

Something familiar comes before me now,

A picture of the Southern cotton-plant.

Broadway to-day, with its white glittering shield,

Is not as pure as Southern cotton field;

    With flakes of snow bursting from bolls of

       green.

Like some imprisoned genius scorning to be

Confined by laws. which bind society,

And breaking bonds is wafted on the breeze

Of public favor, or gathered by the slaves

      Of Fashion. whose vile hands

        Pollute its purity.

True. fragments now and then

Are gently taken to the hearts of men—

White flowers of fancy oftimes sink to rest

Deep in the wells of some fair maiden's breast:

Pure in themselves, they yet become more fair

By contact with the holy thoughts in there.

Cotton and slaves, 'twas thus we counted gold,

The slaves are free, the free in bondage sold;

And now some man with rare prolific brains,

Genius inventive, by the name of Gaines,

Has made a bitters of the cotton plant;

Polluting thus the hitherto white name

By clothing it in the vile badge of shame.

White, glaring white, is all the earth below,

And Broadway seems a " universe of snow."

Or like the Ocean's silver-crested waves,

Upon whose breasts thousands of barks are

    tossed ;

Some brave the storm,—by cautious pilots

    mann'd,

Some strike on breakers, ere they reach the

    land,

      And are forever lost.

E'er yet the sun his quarter's course had run,

Buyers and sellers their day's work begun.

Behind the counter patiently they toil,

      Nor mingle with the busy passing throng ;

Save here and there, an eager care-faced man,

Who wiping cold dew from his tortured brow,

Seeks " Wall," to borrow wherewithal to pay

The rude, insulting, taunting, clamorous crew,

Who all-importunate demand their due.

Teachers of truth, now with the throng pass by,

Some hypocrites, with sanctimonious air,

Sin in their hearts, upon their faces prayer.

Preaching the truth, and living but a lie,

Make me repeat this maxim ever good—

" I am more afraid of Error in the guise of

          Truth,

Than Truth in garb of Error." (9)

Brave was the man, his heart was pure and

strong,

Who, from the pulpit, said the world was wrong

To clothe the Prodigal in direst shame,

And bless the brother with a stainless name.

'Tis to the dying that the doctors give

The healing potion, that will make them live.

No, not the righteous did Christ come to save,

The weak need courage, not the strong and

brave.

He passes now, upon his face a smile

That faces wear, when hearts are free from

guile.

" Church of the strangers," ([10]) I have watched

thy growth,

Have seen thee from a mustard seed spring

forth,

And in thy towering majesty arise,

Until thy spreading branches touched the skies.

All honor be to him whose tender care

Has raised the sapling to a tree so fair.

And " Norwood's " author, whose great study's

man

Seems seeking on this thoroughfare to find

Some subject for his mighty mind

   To dwell upon—

With which to charm the senses of the millions

Who throng to hear him, for he's Fashion's

   " rage,"

As one will be, who makes his church a theatre,

   His pulpit but a stage.

Religion in this wise, enlightened day,

   Is free to all, that is, if all have gold;

The vilest sinner is absolved for pay,

   And to him wide the grand church-doors unfold.

But woe to him who fain would enter in

The gilded fold, whose poverty's his sin.

Now is the Hall clock on the stroke of One;

The Sultans of the journalistic art,

Some without brains, and many without heart,

Come forth to lord it, and in one short hour

The City 'll quake beneath its ruling power.

The daily press,

Whose influence is almighty,

Then it should

Feed greedy masses, with the pure and good,

Not gather like the great Jove-headed Wood,

The daily slander, or the last sensation,

Showing our shame to every foreign nation.

He's for the South! what care I if he is,

Good can be found here, we have evil South.

      The MAN I honor for his love of **right**

And justice, but my truthful muse

Can give no merit to the " Evening News."

The " Evening Mail " I grant an honored place

In the home circle, for its columns bear

Naught save the pure, no badge of our disgrace,

Nothing that Age or Youth would blush to see,

      or hear.

The Poet editor, (¹¹) whose graceful rhyme

Touches the heart like the soft, sweet chime

    Of memory bells, approaches now.

His hair is silvered by the hand of Time.

But his eyes still beam with the youth sublime

That wells from the heart : the poetic fire

That lives, and lives, through years and years,

Whose brightness is dimmed not by joys nor

    tears.

Ah ! now I see in the passing throng

A " prophet and poet," our " king of song,"(¹²)

The bard of Erin, as brave and true

A " Private," as ever wore the blue,

Whose bright lights of genius most brilliantly

        shine,

When kindled on altar of love and—wine.

Now comes a white-haired man with mild and

        lamb-like face,

Kind, gentle eyes, who bears an honored name,

        Beloved by friend, revered by even foe,

Wields the pen-sceptre with majestic grace, (13)

        Who, by example, soothed a people's hate,

And saved a nation from the cursing woe

And bitter shame of striking conquered foe—

Was once a farmer's lad in the old " Granite

    State."

The hardy sons of stern New England's soil,

Taught from their birth to fear not want, nor

    toil,

Bear not the marks of the most dire disease

That Southerners inherit,—love of ease

Well, times have changed, the galling chain

      That made the black man bow

Subservient to a master's mighty will,

      Is broken for Eternity ;

And with that chain the cord that bound

Our Southern souls in idleness to earth.

Wealth earned by others, strown with lavish

hand,

With but one power, the power to command,

Is loosed.

And on Ambition's wings our eager soul

Can reach the mount, Ambition's much-prized

goal.

And grasping to our hearts the spectre Fame,

We faint to find the goddess but a name.

Dreaming again! Ah, how the memory clings

To the dead past : a touch but opes the door

Of the dim vista of departed years,

And phantoms of our hopes and fears,

   In dreamy indistinct array,

Seem flitting up and down this snowy way.

A loaded wagon now, has op'd the door—

"Wilcox and Gibbs'" machine—and nothing

   more. (¹⁴)

Now, I am in the sunny land of flowers,

And smell the perfume from the jasmine bowers;

By opened window sit I half my days,

Sewing the while, but stopping oft to gaze

At two bright fairies, who with sable friends

Hide, like the pixies,

Underneath the petals of some bright flower,

Whose clear celestial hue

My darlings shame, with their bright eyes of

blue.

They crown each other with the garlands fair,

The "grey-beard" mingles with their silken

hair

Like cords of silver, with the jet and gold,

Soft tiny hands are resting on my brow,

I too am crowned:

" I would have made your wreath of white,"

The eldest says, "you are so good,

But, mother, sister said that you were true,

And so we added all these violets blue."

My good machine partaking of my pride

Sang one sweet song, and made the stitches fine,

Making the children hers as well as mine.

'Tis half-past one, and now is seen

In countless numbers eager "limbs of law"

Wending their way to "Courtlandt" from "Nas-

sau,"

To while away an hour with "Smith and

Green." [15]

Their minds to fortify, with meat and drink,

Ex necessitate rei. to enable them to think.

Law! say, what is the law but power?

The strongest mind will rule the hour.

Right. justice. mercy. ah! where are they now?

Not in this land, or, if here, bound in chains.

And only loosed by the command of law,

To whose decree, howe'er unjust we bow,

In meek submission low.

This science intricate we trace

E'en to the dwelling place

Of our first parents;

Children of nature, and of God,

   They knew not there was sin

'Till Satan, in a lawyer's garb,

   Their Eden entered, and with him the light

   Or power of knowing wrong from right.

But, like his children of the present day.

By statements colored in a *legal* way,

And well instilled into his client's mind

By the rare subtleties of lore profound,

Sowing his seed into prolific ground.

He made the white black, and the darkness

      light,

Changed Adam's day into eternal night

By causing wrong appear to be the right :

   And ever thus, as serpents charm they, when

   They cast their glamour on the eyes of men,

   And their each word's a snare,—

   Of Lawyers then, ye innocent, beware !

This world's a stage, each mortal acts a part

Of life's deep tragedy. A breaking heart

Is often hid beneath a smiling face.

Ye, over righteous, if this world's a stage,

Why scorn the mimic copy of life's page ?

Sermons are preached to touch the hearts of men:

No sermon ever moved my heart, as when

I heard sweet " Fanchon," on her bended
       knee, (¹⁶)
Sending above to the kind Deity
      A maiden's holy prayer;
        And then and there
I too prayed that the ray divine
Within my sinful heart should shine.

Oft have I seen the eye of age grow dim
At the mere attitude of homeless " Rip." (¹⁷)
No temperance lecturer could call the vow
Which once burst forth in passionate impulsive-
      ness,

From one who heard the play.

" Never, oh never, shall e'en the smallest sip,

So help me God, again pollute my lip

    Of aught that will intoxicate !"

Surely the spirits which surround us rise

And register such vows above the skies.

Now comes a spirit brave, I ween,

Who on the theater's board is queen,

But on this tragic stage of life,

When kinsmen were at war and strife,

    An angel ministering became. (18)

In sable robes she stood by beds of death,

Wiped the death dews, and caught the latest

breath

Of the brave boys in blue,

Who are sleeping now in the silent grave,

That o'er all the land one flag might wave.

It waves—but its folds are dyed with the

blood

Of the murdered martyrs, the brave, the true,

Who wore the GREY. and who wore the BLUE !

" Physician, heal thyself!" I fain would cry

To those devoted to the healing art.

Who in vast numbers now are passing by :

Is there one wise enough to heal

A wound in his own heart?

Can healing potions which the Doctors give

Imbue the fainting with a wish to live?

Can one relieve the sleepless nights of pain,

Ambition's meed, the torture of the brain

That ever grasps beyond, above, so high,

That all its efforts prove, alas! in vain,

And weary, sinking to the earth,

It curses hour that gave it birth,

Dies, or becomes insane?

There comes an old, well known slouch hat,

Which hides no slouching soul beneath its

    shade, (19)

But one whose greatest power lies

In curing body by first healing mind.

Did they not know when the immortal Davis lay

    Within his prison cell,

That the Leach's skill was not in drugs,

Who healed and made him well ?

They knew not, who the power of speech denied,

    Of histories in touch of hands ;

    Of volumes in a glance.

How could they know ? formed of earth's com-

    mon clay,

Of the magnetic cords which bind

The thoughts of those whose natures are refined,

Whose bodies are subservient to the mind.

Strange, how a mortal by the power of will

  And genius, tho' untutored can exalt

Himself, until he will appear

  A being from another sphere,

As unlike to the common throng

As rhyming jingle to a stately song.

Few days ago, I heard kind blessings showered

  Upon his head who now draws near :[20]

Who had opened the once closed portals

    Of a soul's doors.

A mother, with a fearful heart,

    Without one ray of hope.

Placed in this Doctor's hands her only child,

Whose beauty needed naught, save sight,

To make it seem an angel bright.

One stifled cry! 'Oh, mother, is this light?

'Twas black before, and, mother, now 'tis

    white.

I see you, mother, and I see God too!'

The little child, with its pure instinct rare,

Felt that God's spirit surely must be there,

For mother taught Light was, at God's command.

And God alone could hold light in His hand.

The seasons change, opinions change,
   And even senses change with time ;
In age we see not with the eyes
   We looked from in our youth's full prime.
Couleur de rose is turned to sober grey,
Which grows more sombre every hour and day ;
   And Fashion too, like all things here below,
Is ever changing, as the sunset cloud ;
First a vast mountain, then a fleecy shroud,

A mass of darkness, now of crimson hue,

Soft, silver-tinted, then a violet blue;

    Then blending all the shades in the rainbow.

Now Fashion's minions, in the last new style,

Pass and repass, disdaining the slight smile

      That curls the lip of ever scornful man,

Whose brains inventive all new styles design,

      From fancy gaiters to arranging hair.

I've studied Nature, and I've studied Art,

Can at a glance detect, in smallest part

Of a grand toilet, whose great Artist's skill,

Moulded the madam to her august will,

If from the fashion-plates of Harper's good

"Bazar," "Die Modenwelt" or "Magazine

Of Madam Demorest," the robes were made.

If the rival artists([21]) of the present day,

Which hold in Fashion's world the sway

    Of reigning queens,

Their wondrous genius used to create

The airy, fairy figures slight,

Which make this city full of light.

I know, if from our "Merchant Prince" was

    bought

The fabric rare, made in a foreign land,

Upon whose very surface seems inwrought

A sightless eye, a wasted, helpless hand

Of some poor wretch, who e'en his senses gave

To deck the garment over which we rave.

Those tasty habits, costly, plain, and neat,

Disclosing 'neath their folds two tiny feet,

Snugly encased in leather-shoes thick soled.

Are snares which catch the unwary heart of

     man ;

Those costly jewels, too, from "Browne and

     Spaulding's" bought—

Are many a lesson to the wedded taught,

That Fanchon bonnet, ribbon and a flower,

Speak to man's pocket with all potent power.

But Fashion, although charming for a while,

Has not the lasting power of a smile.

Broadway! all glorious and grand, the city's

     heart;

A panorama! on the changing scene I gaze

     With reverential awe.

Work of man's hand—proof of a mortal's skill,

Who moulds such structures to his mighty will.

Once, where the "Herald" palace stands,

The red man claimed his home and lands.

One hundred years ago Hans smoked at ease

On summer eve, beneath the sheltering trees

Which grew where now the " Leader," " Tri-

bune," " World,"

Is daily, weekly, to our gaze unfurled,

Sending abroad the city's different views

Of national affairs.

Where stands the office of the Surrogate and

" Times,"

A church-bell pealed its sweet and solemn

chimes,

Not twenty years ago.

So the huge building rears its stately head

Above the city of the sainted dead.

Thrice haunted spot! for when the Hall clock

Strikes the hour of ten each night,

One gifted with a two-fold sight

Can witness scenes, scenes so appalling, drear,

That common souls would faint to even hear.—

First comes the red man, brandishing in air

His tomahawk, showing despair

    Upon his dusky face ;

Then, with triumphant stare,

He waves above his head the hair,

Dripping with gore, of newly murdered foe.

His pale wife follows, and a sad surprise

Rests on her face, and in her mournful eyes,

They seem to miss the grand old forest trees,

And with the wail, " No home ! no place of

rest !"

They vanish as they came.

Fantastic forms in dress of olden times

Enter at will, through each self-opening door,

Or oft arise in seeming through the floor.

Chanting with solemn voices, old sweet hymns;

Such good old tunes, as in the days of yore

Made echoes ring from hill-side, and from shore.

Old wrinkled dames,—men in their manhood's

prime,

And round-faced maidens, with their locks of

        night,

Their crimson cheeks, and eyes so full of light,

Linger a moment, and then fade away.

Men robed in later styles the dark halls fill,

Hold eager consultation; then a thrill

Of indignation seems to move the mass.

And to the office of the Surrogate ([22]) they

        throng,

In a chill current, like the whirlwind strong—

And eagerly they seek, in each small nook to

        find

Some traces of the WILL they left behind.

Some smiling faces look upon me now,

But many glance, with a dark lowering brow,

Upon the fragments of a broken will.

In deep sepulchral tones, amid the ghostly din,

A stern voice utters, " Bring the culprit in."

    And the last Surrogate

Is ushered in, and takes his chair of state;

Grim Death is standing by his head,

And o'er him spirits of the happy dead

    Are keeping watch.

Orphans and widows, with all patience wait

To hear the verdict of the Surrogate.

He tears the *will*, declares 'tis Law's command,

And in a moment all the ghostly band

Have vanished, save the solemn clerk

Who writes until earth's pall of night

Is changed for robes of glorious light.

Shadows on the snow are lying,

Day is dead, the year is dying;

Wailing winds around are sighing

For the year that now is dying.

Tell me, year, before thy fleeting,

Tell me what will be the greeting

Of the year we'll soon be meeting,

Are the hopes that fill me, cheating?

Old year, whisper—still I listen!

Are hopes only drops that glisten

For a moment, as they christen

      Rose-buds newly born?

And the old year tells me. dying,

In the voice of winds soft sighing—

" Child of earth, cease, cease thy crying,

      What is life but hope?

Old year, give me e'er thy leaving

Token, that I may cease grieving ;

Make my faith pure, keep me believing

  Both in man and God.

Silver clouds are o'er me sailing,

And the strickened year fast paling,

Softly whispers 'mid the wailing—

  "I leave thee LOVE and HOPE."

N O T E S.

As this Book is expected to have considerable circulation outside the limits of the City, it has been suggested that a few Notes be appended, explanatory of the localisms contained therein :—

NOTE 1.

Loew's, or as it is commonly called, Fulton Street Bridge, was completed March, 1866, the building being supervised by the Hon. Charles E. Loew, whose name has been bestowed upon it by an Act of the Common Council of New York.

It is a large aerial structure, at the intersection of Broadway and Fulton Street, where the thoroughfare is continually thronged with vehicles of all kinds, rendering it almost impossible for pedestrians to pass.

NOTE 2.

Only for readers not familiar with New York would it be necessary to say, that this refers to the Police.

NOTE 3.

Wall Street is our temple of Mammon, where men of money "most do congregate."

NOTE 4.

This is no fancy sketch. The writer actually saw this,— saw a Southern soldier give alms to the Northern soldier, who can be seen at any time near the Bridge playing an organ. Indeed everything described was seen, if not precisely in the order mentioned.

NOTE 5.

It is but common justice to say that this manly sentiment is reported of the Hon. John Morrissey.

NOTE 6.

Hon. John T. Hoffman is Mayor of New York at this writing, November 11th, 1867.

NOTE 7.

And the Hon. Fernando Wood, the rival candidate for the Mayoralty.

NOTE 8.

Always at the Bridge are venders selling the dancing toys, whose motions depend upon an elastic string. the invention of which has brought a fortune to the inventor.

NOTE 9.

This quotation is from Rev. Dr. Deems, and the allusion to " the prodigal," refers to a sermon preached by Dr. Deems, in which he represents the elder brother as worse than the prodigal. A report of that discourse, which produced a great impression on its delivery, appears in " Every Month," for September, published by S. T. Taylor.

NOTE 10.

"The Church of the Strangers," the name of a congregation composed of persons of all denominations, mostly strangers in New York; and its pastor, Dr. Deems, is abundant in labors among the sick, the poor, and the prisoner, and those who have no friends. It gives the author pleasure to say a word for an enterprise so catholic and so beneficial.

NOTE 11.

Perhaps it is superfluous to mention the name of the venerable William C. Bryant, of the "Evening Post."

NOTE 12.

"Miles O'Reilly" is the well known name of Gen. Charles G. Halpine, who is justly called our "King of Song," and who has written certain beautiful things, which will be remembered long after his career as a politician shall have been forgotten.

NOTE 13.

With whatever power Hon. Horace Greeley does anything, the wielding of the pen is the only thing he is accused of doing "with grace."

NOTE 14.

The "Wilcox and Gibbs' sewing machine," celebrated

alike for its simplicity, rapidity of movement, as well as its durability, was patented in 1857, first sold in 1859, since which time one hundred thousand have been sold.

NOTE 15.

A well known and excellent restaurant in Cortlandt street.

NOTE 16.

Maggie Mitchell, the fascinating actress, has made this character memorable.

NOTE 17.

Play-goers will always know Joe Jefferson by his remarkable impersonation of " Rip Van Winkle."

NOTE 18.

Mrs. Gen. Lander, our American actress, is believed to surpass Ristori in the character of Elizabeth. Her goodness

is equal to her greatness, as her attentions to the soldiers
during the war demonstrates.

NOTE 19.

Dr. J. J. Craven, the physician attendant on Jefferson
Davis at Fortress Monroe, and author of "Prison Life
of Davis."

NOTE 20.

This actually occurred in the practice of Edward B.
Foote, M.D., the celebrated medical and electrical the-
rapeutist, and author of "Medical Common Sense."

NOTE 21.

The artists referred to, are Madams M. F. Gillespie and
Demorest, whose exquisite taste has rendered them renowned
in the fashionable circles, not only of New York, but of
the whole United States.

NOTE 22.

Hon. Gideon J. Tucker, who has held important State offices for more than twenty years, and is one of the first political writers of the age, is the present Surrogate of New York, and has occupied that position for the last five years. It is said of him that he has never been politically wrong in his life.